I0743076

From Selkirk to Sagebrush

Eileen Bell

In fervent dreams
the wee birdie sings,
and the wild flowers spring,
and in sunshine the waters sleeping,
but the broken heart it kens,
nae second Spring again.

Fifth verse of Loch Lomond

From Selkirk to Sagebrush

Eileen Bell

The events of this story were inspired by events in my ancestor's lives, but the people and the circumstances in the story are fictional.

Copyright Eileen Bell 2021

ISBN: 978-1-989092-55-2

Published by Celticfrog Publishing
Kamloops, B.C. Canada

Part One
CNR Train Station-Kamloops BC.

Passengers are scattered across the large room. Near the top of the wall, a small window is open midway across the room. An afternoon breeze drifts lazily through the window, carrying with it, a whiff of warm late summer air and beyond a chilly stillness from the Thompson river. A pretty dark-haired girl in a bonnet, a long dress and thin coat sits alone on the bench by the far corner wall. She is reading a book and occasionally glances at her watch. A silver ring glints on the middle finger of her left hand.

Brothers, Henry and Arthur, and two younger boys, bustle through the swinging door of the station hauling their cases and bags. Arthur ducks his head through the doorway and then trips over his bag. Henry reaches out a hand to help but Arthur pushes him away. Henry steps back and laughs, brushing a dark lock of hair away from his forehead and grins slyly at his brother

"Ur ye looking at that lass across the room then Arthur?" sneers Stewy. "Better watch where those feet Are steppin' or the pretty lasses will nae be comin' your way."

"Ah-ah. Stop yer jaggering then. The door rise is ju-just too low for the likes a' me is a-all."

Fred chimes in. "He havin' his knickers in a knot for the lassies alright."

Fred chortles. "That stutterin' will nae help 'im either."

"Ah. Shut yer gobs! Henry points toward the benches. What are you doing standin' around the door? Go park ye butts ye' willy nits."

The boys scramble over each other and their belongings in their haste to be the first to the long straight-backed bench in the middle of the room.

Henry stays by the door, peering through a nearby window. The light breeze from the high window wafts a slightly dank smell from the river. The mountains overhead are mostly treeless, but peaceful in their barrenness.

"I wonder what that yellow carpet-like stuff is, growing on the mountain's surface. I be bettin' the summer sun il' burn down from those bare mountains on the town. Not much growin' in hills t' take in the heat. Wheat fields in the valley where we be workin' must be baskin' in heat an' ripe for harvest.

Mr. Holmes, emerges disheveled, from the steam train that has carried them from the coastal port of Vancouver. He passes through the door and walks by Henry without a glance sideways and hurries toward the scattered boys.

"Now my boys," he harps after them. "Slow down, slow down."

As he hurries along Mr. Holmes brushes absent crumbs from his shirt and runs his fingers through his hair.

Henry watches from beside the station entrance. *Holmes- He tries so hard at times to be in charge, but, ach, he's makin' a muck of it.*

He sees Mr. Holmes raise his hands in the air; then falter like an absent-minded, orchestra conductor who's forgotten his tempo. Then Mr. Holmes recalls his instructions for the boys.

"We've a bit to wait, boys, for the train to Ashcroft. It's a short ride. and we shall be there before nightfall. We'll have to walk along from the station to the ranch, but we'll have time to set up out tents outside before dark. Take your seats and I shall purchase our tickets."

Arthur and the two boys sprawl across the bench. Henry walks over and sits close to Fred. He pushes against his back and shoulders to force him to sit up.

The girl in the corner glances over at the unruly group, then looks away quickly.

"The wee lass is spottin' ye again Arthur," Fred smirks, looking straight ahead, as he grudgingly sits up.

He pushes against Henry's chest to shove him away. "Don't be sittin' on me ye hefty gruff. "

Fred pokes Arthur in the side with his elbow.

"She likes how you been so gracefully fallin' a' ower yer feet. Ye daft, clumsy oaf."

"S'no Arthur who's getting her attention," Henry,

raises his head to direct Fred's gaze across the room.

They all stare across the room. Mr. Holmes is chatting with the young woman and has her full attention.

Henry puts his hand to his lips to quiet the boys, so he can hear what Holmes and the girl are saying. He shakes his head in disbelief.

Mr. Holmes walks slowly past the girl sitting on the bench. He looks towards her with a friendly nod and a smile. She looks up from her book.

"Mr. Holmes is it? May I talk with you a minute, Sir? You are from the borderlands in Scotland. You have traveled a long way. You and all your charges must be weary and needing a meal and a good night's rest."

Is he flirting with that young lass? Who is she tae him? Why doesn't he look after these lads as is his duty- his job- as their schoolmaster? Why am I always left seein' to these luddy louts? Is that why he was beggin' Arthur and me to come along on this trip? So I canna' do his job for him? On the train from Vancouver he sat up front and chatted with other passengers. He nae said a word to any of us the whole time and just now he come past the station door without even seein' I was about.

"I am here to welcome you to Kamloops and accompany you and your young men on the train to Ashcroft this evening," the young woman continues.

"Yes," Mr. Holmes answers, as he sits carefully

beside her on the bench. "Still-Water Inn?" You must be the daughter of Jack Still-Water. Your father, does he own and operate the Inn as well as the ranch of the same name? Such a pretty young lady- May I ask your name?"

"Margaret, Margaret Still-Water. I have several older brothers and sisters. My sisters are married and are busy with their own families and my brothers are helping with ranch duties and operations, so I am left to manage the Inn. I do enjoy the day to day hustle and bustle and like to make my own decisions and as long as the Inn is profitable, I'll keep doing that."

"That's mighty fine, Miss Still-Water."

"With your permission, Mr. Holmes, I would like to give you and the boys dinner and a bed free of charge tonight at the Still-Water Inn. This is my welcoming gift."

"I am most delighted with your offer. Why not call me Jack, Jack Holmes it is? He smiles as he reaches to shake her small, gloved hand. I shall inform the boys immediately. They will be so pleased not to have to spend their first night inland in a drafty tent."

Mr. Holmes laughs at his own weak attempt at humor, then a blush creeps across his face as Margaret fails to laugh. She nods and smiles politely.

Now, Henry sees Holmes, strutting along, excited with his own importance, hurrying towards the bench.

I dinae care if she has invited us tae spend the night at her Inn. He's a fool.

"Holmes be damned!" he spews for all in earshot.

He stands flush in Holmes' face to prevent him from taking a seat.

"What are you up tae Holmes?"

"Henry? Pardon me?" Holmes steps back.

"Getting polite now 'ur ye? He jabs a finger into Holmes chest. "Goin' tae sit with her on the train, aye? Ye so-oo polite when ye bein' up tae no good."

He waves his arms crazily in Mr. Holmes face. His words fly from his mouth, so quickly he hardly knows what's passing his lips.

Henry only half hears the boys snickering.

"I'm no goin' with ye tae the hay field or the Inn or whatever plans yer makin'."

"I was just about to say--"

"Dinae fret yerself"

Henry grabs his bag and tumbles through the swinging door. A few drops of rain pucker against his thin coat. He sinks down and crouches against the corner of the station wall.

"Wha' am I goin' to do now?"

The raindrops splash off his hardened leather boots. Henry rubs his face and smacks his fist against his forehead. The rain falls harder now soaking through his pant legs. He looks up from his soggy outpost. Raindrops slide along to the end of the overhang and down to the ground. As he steps out, rain splatters down his neck. He reaches to wipe away the water and then backs into the flank of a large stallion tied to a hitching post, in front of the station. The horse snorts and raises his front legs and then his back haunches in the air. Henry grabs the bridle and pulls down on it to try to settle him, but the stallion raises upper body and snorts once again, shaking his head and mane. Henry speaks softly to the horse, while pulling down on the bridle once more.

"Settle m' lad. Ye doin' fine. Just me's the clumsy fellow."

Henry steps back, but too late, as the horse comes down, with his front left hoof onto Henry's right foot. Henry backs away and stumbles across the train yard, up the slight hill and onto a wide street.

Nothing's goin' right today. The damn horse, he's got it in for me too.

The signpost reads "Lorne Street." Lining the street are several tar-paper shacks and two sturdier looking wooden buildings with fenced yards behind, which housed assorted animals. There were fields of stubby grass and sagebrush in between. He walks with his head down, his shoulders hunched against the rain, dragging his injured foot behind. A donkey brays from someone's backyard as he walks by. The bray makes him startle and jerk his head up. He sees a bench ahead, limps over and sits heavily, loosening his boot, he examines his injury. He removes his one bloody sock. It is cut, bruised and beginning to swell, but he sees no bones out of place. He puts his foot back in his sock and eases his boot back on. He ties his lace loosely. A rooster crows in the distance. Sitting on the bench, he remembers the last conversation he and Arthur had with their Father, who was the Anglican Minister for Selkirk and the surrounding county. Henry had wanted his father to understand why he and Arthur wished to take this trip to Canada. The conversation hadn't gone well.

***

Henry clears his throat and looks directly at his father-Charles. Henry is trying to quiet his rising anxiety.

"We know ye been thinkin' and wantin' to ask about our plans, now we have our school- leaving papers. We plannin' to go along with Mr. Holmes, the schoolmaster and two school-boys to help with the September hayin' in a place called Ashcroft in BC.'s interior. As you ken, I like the outdoor work and Arthur - Arthur can speak for himself."

Henry could see now from this rain-soaked bench in this dusty, small town far across the ocean, how things had begun to go wrong. Arthur never did speak up much for himself. At least not in a manner that convinced Father to let them have their way. Arthur just spoke, not thinking about how Father or anyone else would react.

"What the devil. Ur ye mad boys? Canada- BC.?"

Arthur looked eagerly at Henry. His admiring expression says he is very sure Henry can persuade their father to allow them to travel on this several month-long, haying trip.

"Nothin' but wild Indians ready with their hatchets or bow and arrows, ready tae scalp the white man. Good Lord! They attack trains. Did ye ever hear the story? What was his name? Bill Miner, but he was a white man from the United States, mind you. Near a place called Kamloops. Something like that. Jumps off a bluff overlooking the track onto the roof of the train and down into the car with his guns out ready tae shoot if the passengers don't give him everything they have. I heard he took all their shoes in one passenger car. And then leaving every decent, white passenger shoe-less, he gave all the footwear-- he gave all white people's shoes to a tribe of Indians. What would they want with lady's heels? Aye, they caught him though. Nasty fellow- by all accounts. There are, of course, decent and hardworking ranchers and cowboys. Been readin' some books about the goings on in Canada. Very uncivilized. I forbid it. Ye not be goin'. Much too dangerous. And Arthur – Arthur-- Ye see what I'm sayin' of course, don't ye?"

Arthur gazes beseechingly at Henry, then back to his father.

"I-I want to go Father. N-no reason not to. We'll be looked after with Mr. Holmes k- keeping an eye on us. It's an adventure you see. And m-mum, she'll have less meals to get and cleanin' to do with us bein' away for a wee while."

"Mother? What do' she have to do with this? Too tied to her apron strings, Arthur. Spending time helpin' your mother in the kitchen. Never seen the like. A big gaffer like you gettin' tangled in your wee mum's skirts.

"I like to help mum,"

Charles ignores Arthur, clears his throat, and looks again at Henry.

"You two ought to be doing men's work, but not way off in the wilds of Canada."

"Awh, Father you got your head stuck inside too many books," Henry chokes back the acid in his throat. He sits up straight in his chair. "'Tis no like it say in tae books. There's good Indians and white folks too. We need to see first hand."

Henry sees now, from his solitary bench, how things had gone wrong. Mr. Holmes had met the boys in the street the next day. He eagerly asked how it went with getting their father's permission to get on the boat to Canada.

"Nae sae good,"

"I'll get you two on that ship from Newcastle. I have your passports. Leaving tomorrow at 9 pm. Meet me here at 10:00 am. I'll be coming with the other boys and a horse and cart. We'll be in Newcastle by nightfall. Bring a wee bit of supper and whatever money you have." He patted Henry on the shoulder, then walked away.

Arthur cracks his knuckles, then runs his hands through his thick, curly red hair.

"It's n-not okay is it? Do you really think we can get father's permission by tomorrow, Henry?"

"Leave it tae me. I'll get us sorted. We'll meet Holmes tomorrow and be on the boat. "

***

The rain has stopped. He tries to walk on the higher ground between the wagon-ruts, but it is slow going with his injured foot. Blood seeps between his toes. The sun is setting across the river and scattering flickers of light across the road. He sees a few seagulls prancing along the shore looking for grubs and a white heron standing on a log out in the river, patiently waiting for his dinner. Henry drags himself through the wet dirt and gravel and across the rise to the station.

A train is pulling away. It belches and hisses as it begins its short journey westward. Clouds of steam obliterates the scene around it. For a few moments Henry is mesmerized by the pulsating dampness of the disappearing train cars.

Damn the likes of it. They're goin' on without me. I be in a right mess now.

Inside the station Arthur is pacing the floor by the wicket. He cracks his knuckles and looks anxiously towards the door, then sees Henry come through the door and breaks into a wide grin.

"I saved ma t-ticket and I got your ticket from M-Mr. Holmes. Knew you'd be back. The Station Master says we can get a train to Ashcroft here in the mornin' He gave me a b-beer."

Henry grabs him in a bear hug and tries lifting him from the ground. He groans with pain and puts Arthur down quickly. "I am glad you waited."

Arthur looks down at his brother's foot. "Wha-goin' on with you? Yer limpin.'"

"Had a run in with a horse tied up outside. He got excited and came down a wee bit hard. Be better tomorrow," he said, lightly laughing.

"Ye have na' break?"

"Nah," he says but winces in pain.

"Holmes was mad, but I told him. I told him I had to wait for ye. Ue pleased with me?"

"Aye- pleased with you Arthur, but not with me-self. I'm such a damn, daft fool for running off and now this," he says as he points to his foot.

"Ah need to learn tae wind in my temper."

"A daft fool." Arthur scoffs and punches Henry in the shoulder. "B-but-- We can sleep in the back room, the Station Master told me. Train leaves at 8 am. We're not sae bad off now, aye? But how will we get to the ra-ranch from the train in the mornin? With yer

limpin' foot and all- that'll be a long stretch."
Arthur leads the way to the back room.
"I' sort it. Never ye mind. I' sort it."

Part Two

Henry can hear Margaret talking through the slightly open door to the back room where he is resting in the Still-Water Inn.

"Yes, You'll have to talk it over with my father. He likes it all to be run by him first."

Then he hears Holmes reply. "Of course my dear, rightly so, rightly so." Henry imagines her wincing slightly at the "My dear." Holmes continues, "So how are you managing with the boys and the extra work."

"Oh," She absently replies, looking down at the register. Henry smiles to himself. Margaret has been kindly tending to his injured foot for the last week while he is laid up in the back room. He sits in a large, overstuffed chair, with his foot resting on a stool and covered with a blanket. A pair of crutches lean against the back of the chair.

Right fool I've been to get myself tangled up and stomped on by the stallion outside the train station in Kamloops, within the first hour of arrivin'. Not startin' out right with me boss, him and me havin' a spat. Ahh- I can hear him still blathering up the wee girl. She's tryin' to get him off. Ah- I hear 'im comin' now.

"Sorry to say-Arthur's a right dobber." Holmes starts in, after a quick hello. "I'm telling you Henry. He's tripping over his feet in the hay field. Like a wagon with three wheels careening round a rocky turn in the road. Wishing you were out helping us. It's the first week of September and we only have til the end of the month to get the hay in. How's the foot healing? Been keeping company with Margaret, I see. She's been tending to you in her spare time."

Henry eyes Holmes suspiciously, as Holmes paces the room, sometimes leaning over Henry, talking and waving his arms upward, as if he could will him to rise and walk straight to the adjacent hay field and begin tossing bales on the wagon, his injured foot miraculously healed. In reality, Henry's foot is covered in a sour, pungent salve and wrapped in a thick bandage. Mr Holmes pinches his nose.

"Whats that? Horse liniment she's swabbed you with?"

"Ahh- Yes… Clears the nose does it not? Like a pile of flavored hay. Gets the eyes runnin' rhummy, but is all she has. Been looking to me as she can. Got an Inn to run and all. Didn't do my foot any kindness to be walkin' them miles to this place after the train journey from Kamloops. Arthur had been trying to keep me movin' along the road, wi' his arm round my shoulder and me draggin' and limpin' behind, dreading bein' laid up an' all on first arrivin.' Mr. Still-Water spots us after a bit, stops and helps me into his posh blue model T. He was lookin' out the road fa' us and was happy when he found out we were the two late lads. Aye, right pleasing to me and Arthur, after our long trudge. I don't recall we'd ever been in a proper car. Here I am now sittin' all day like a pointless penny-waster."

"I have an idea that might help. I know you'll be somewhat injured for the rest of haying season. You could sit atop the hay-wagon. You could direct the haying from the wagon. Maybe yer gawf of a brother will listen to your direction."

"Arthur ain't no gawf. Watch it Holmes."
Before Holmes could reply, Henry added. "You want me to sit on-top a rickety hay wagon and bark orders to the crew. Stupid, daft is what it is. Oh, I see. You want me who is hurtin' to direct hayin' while ye be lazin' about at the Inn."

"Ahh. Well-I say- I do have paperwork to send home. Letting the backers; you know the farmers back home whose shillings we've been travelling on know the situation. You being laid up and so on. How much hay has been cut and stoked since our arrival last week? How we're all getting on."

"Yer the head gaffer Holmes, but I hope yer not stokin' that hay before its dry. Whose doin' the rakin'?"

Holmes is puzzled for a moment and then answers. "Raking, Aye of course- yes, no slacking."

"Whose the dobber now, Holmes, Ya dinae been

dryin' the hay proper long enough after rakin' have ye'?" Henry speaks before Holmes has a chance to reply. "Why d' ye no put Arthur on the rakin'? He likes tasks he can do slow and careful. Hay has to dry most days at least two hours after it's raked before its pitched onto wagon or stoked. I think ya may be movin' a bit too fast in the hay-field. Hope yer pitchin' a few dozen forks over the fence. Extra bit for them cattle over the next fence if the grass turns poorly."

" Yes yes, Quite right you are my boy. Holmes voice sounds more upbeat than he looks. "Why don't you get out in the field and give it a go?"

Henry knows Holmes is not much interested in gettin' the hay and is wantin' to be spendin' his time elsewhere than in the hay field, as in the Inn, chatting up Margaret.

"I'll sit on the end of the hay-wagon for a bit and See how it goes. I be out tomorrow. I be kickin' tha boys from their bunkhouse early. Better give em' a warnin.' Only one condition Holmes; Arthur bunks in with me from now on. Don't want them boys raggin' 'im. Let Arthur know he'll be beddin' with me. Send a wagon for Arthur n' me at six am. Now leave me be. Be needing my bed soon with all y' chaffin' at me."

"See you then tomorrow. You're a good man Henry."

"I' the head gaffer now. Yer damn right."

Holmes hesitates before leaving through the back door. "I'll be letting Mr. Still-water know the arrangements."

Henry waves him away and mutters. *Proper polite fool when he wants something. So now I'm a man, am I. Few minutes ago I was just a lad. I'll be bettin' he's no gettin' the hay in right.*

***

Holmes does as Henry bids him and brings the two horses hitched to the hay wagon at six am the next morning. As it is too early to disturb anyone, Holmes makes his way back to his cabin. His is a small tidy cabin which is about 100 yards behind the much rougher sleeping quarters of Stewy and Fred and the seasonal hired- help.

Arthur drives the hay wagon to pick up the boys. The field that faces the main road leading into Ashcroft is their working hay field. Arthur has never driven a wagon before, so Henry gives Arthur some tips.

"Just keep 'em at a steady trot. Aach,' Wa' no goin' tae the races."

"I be l-learnin' l-lots from you. Now you be lookin' after us out there. Holmes was gettin' a-after me for not c-cutting the hay right. I told him he had to d-dry the hay after c-cutting and rakin' for at least two hours d-depending on the weather. Pleased yer comin' along now. Y' want to be c-caref-ful yer no be hurtin' yer foot again."

"Yer so right about the hay and m' foot, Arthur. W' hae it sorted, Never you mind."

"Yer a-always sayin' that, ma' brother- s-s-somet-time a' nay work out like we t-thinkin'." Arthur laughs.

Henry tosses Arthur a grim smile.

" Brother, smarter than you look. I missed you brother."

" M-missed you too," Arthur answers, smiling happily. Distracted by their show of affection, he slackens the reins and one of the horses veers off the road.

22

"Don't go gawpy-eyed. Be keepin' em' reined."

Arthur pulls back on the reins.

"I'm doing good. D-doing good."

"Yes you are, let's be gettin' on. No muckin' about."

Henry draws a deep breath of the cool morning air and looks up at the sun rising behind the fuzzy, stretching hills.

"Nice to be outside again Arthur. A beautiful bit a' country. It's been a right dreary week cooped up inside the Inn."

To himself he thinks. *It wa'nt so dreary when Margaret was around. Holmes was right about that part.*

As they arrive at the bunkhouse, the boys stumble unwashed and bleary-eyed, from the door to greet Arthur and Henry.

" Get yerselves a wash- no slackin'," he says pointing to the hand pump a short distance away. "Sun will be bakin' our backsides soon. Make lively. Kitchen's packed us a meal." Henry throws the lunch to Fred. "Mind ya' two don't chaw it down before we get a bite in later." Fred catches the lunch before it falls in the dirt.

"G' off wi' ye- wiping at yer faces. Hoist inna' back a' the wagon. "Don't get yer knickers in knots. I ain't comin' to help with the work in field as yet. I'll be watchin' you from the wagon to see things are goin' as the boss likes em. In a bit when I'm healed right, l' be down in the field with you forkin' stokes and makin' sure cattle are fed a share of hay. Arthur will be on the rakin' for now. You two yer' on cuttin.' Two men from the village will be coming later wi' a horse and mower tae be startin' with cuttin' and rakin' the field in back. Yer scythes be sharp, I hope. Let's get on then."

Later that afternoon Henry leans against a hay bale propped against the corner of the fence. He wipes sweat from his brow, with the back of his arm and sips from a flask of lemonade. Arthur is carefully raking out the hay the mowers had just finished cutting.

Standing and swinging the scythe in the air, Fred looks over at Henry.

"Why ya' givin' him the easy job and we be on cuttin' since early morning? Makin' a pet a' yer brother, so wi' seein."

"Yer gawpin' dobbers' stealin' the easy job," Stewy chimes in.

"Watch as how yer swingin' that tool there, Fred. Y' two boys be needin' to watch yer mouths. If ye don't like it, put yer scythes down an' be goin' back to yer bunkhouse and don't bother comin' to work tomorrow. See what kind of a pay packet you'll be gettin' at the end of the month. An' if either of ye' thinkin' to speak rough again wi' Arthur er' me ye be sittin' suckin' yer gums in the bunkhouse. Be off wi' ye."

Without another word Stewy and Fred chucked

their tools against the fence and ran off.

"Ya' told em' dinna' ye Henry?"

"Acch, Never mind, Arthur, back to the rakin' before the rain starts spittin'."

"There ain't no rain. Look a' the sk-sky."

"You mind me. I ye boss now? If I be sayin' the rains a comin', it be."

" Sometime rain comin'." Arthur says in a muffled sing- song voice and smiling to himself, as he carefully rakes the fresh cut hay.

After two more weeks of hard work, the harvesters were given two full days off before the final week of haying.

****

Henry is relaxing in the chair in the back of the Inn. Arthur talks to Henry as he tidied up the room. Henry's foot is still slightly swollen and he couldn't yet put much weight on it but he is feeling good because the hay is mostly in and his foot was healing well enough. He still has to rely on crutches to get around.

"What if Margaret comes by. She dinae w' to be seein' yer room in a mess here. Y' like her Henry?"
"Ach,' good lass."
" I be thinkin' you like her Henry."
"Go on- Get off will y.' Yer' the bloke is cleaning up for her."
Henry changes the subject. "How'd you like to write to mum and father?"
"I can tell 'em I be drivin' the hay- wagon and the rakin' and waterin' ta' cattle. They be right proud. Father w- won't be gettin' on us f' going to Canada with all the wor-rk we been doin'. An' we' be get-ting paid and goin' on the boat and goin' home the end of the m- month. We didn't see nae w-wild Ind-dians neither."

"Wha,' you think Father's upsettin hi'self?" He looks at his hands. They were cold and clammy.

Arthur says nothing, but looks at Henry with a curious knowing in his eyes.

Henry has already written the first part of the letter. He'd apologized to his parents about the way he left Selkirk without saying goodbye and leaving without permission. Worst thing of all in his mind was he'd taken his mum's kitchen money. He admitted all these mistakes in the letter home- How sorry he was, but he focused mostly on how well Arthur is doing.

In a couple of days they would begin the final push to get the hay in. Henry has an eerie feeling he couldn't quite put a finger on. Going home is almost unreal to him. He feels in some strange way he belongs right where he is in the interior of BC., in the high-desert ranching/ farmland of the Thompson Valley.

Margaret is taking a day off and Mr. Holmes is also nowhere to be seen. Henry can hear muffled voices from the dining room.

"Must be servin' Sunday lunch. Like to get me some of that good smelling roast lamb. Lots a' sheep farmin' round here too, Arthur. Like to go lookin' round the area a bit."

"Ye na goin' out til' that foots healed up.

"Maybe we could be takin' the horse and wagon," Henry mocks, knowing Arthur would say nae.

"Acch- A-a-another time-a-another time. Why do ye' wan' to do a daft t-thing like that with a hurtin' foot."

Henry didn't answer.

He is thinking about Margaret. They'd had some good conversations in the evenings after the hired help and Holmes had finished with their supper and the Inn was finally quiet. Arthur usually would offer to help with the washing up after supper.

I do find it hard to focus when she gets to tellin' me

The boys finish the letter and are sealing it in the
envelope when Holmes walks in in a jovial mood.

"Writing home. Good lads. I just been out and
about with Margaret and her father. We drove round
looking about at farms and businesses. Stopping at a
few to make polite inquiries. Seems like a hardworking, prosperous little valley. Did you know they
started up a farmers' association a few years back?
Started in Kamloops, I believe. Many of the--"

Henry interrupted. "You been out with Margaret
and Mr. Still-Water?"

"Oh, the look on your face, my lad. Shall I get
you a mirror?"

To rub it in, Holmes adds, "It's Jack Still-Water.
First name basis is best for a good afternoon chat."

" Accch- Gi' off wi' ya, Holmes. Ye bein' a right
ass."

Realizing he had gone too far, Holmes adds, "I'll
ask Margaret to look in on you." He can't hide the
traces of a smirk.

"Acch... A' ring the bell if I need. Off wi' ye." He

28

waves Holmes away.

"I'll post the letter for you. I have letters from the younger boys to post as well. Postman is due tomorrow at ten. I'll give it to him straight away."

Henry put the letter in his hand, more to be rid of the man, than for any feeling of gratitude.

Henry sighs and looks towards the slightly open door, which leads to the main part of the Inn.

Arthur speaks up. "I going to help in the k-kitchen with g-gettin' supper on the table. Stewy, Fred and the others will be here soon for their e-evenin' meal. Y' alright, brother?"

"Aye good." He smiled fondly at Arthur. "Go get them wee plates on the table. I'm wishin' to be gettin' my supper in here tonight. Dinae like seein'-- you know?"

"Holmes," says Arthur shrugging his shoulders, then he turns down the hallway to the kitchen.

***

Margaret brings Henry his supper. She stands beside his chair.

"Sorry about the missed outing. We drove into town. Mr. Holmes had to pick up a parcel at the train station. We dropped him off and picked him up later. He horn-swoggled my father."

Henry looks puzzled. "Wha' ye mean- horn- what-swag- erwoggled?"

Margaret laughs. "If you've got your arm gripped around the neck of a calf and your other hand grabbing its horns it's not going anywhere without you."

"Good description, that's rancher talk. I' be gettin' to learnin' some a' that talk."

Henry notices a shy blush creeping across Margaret's cheek. She steps back and sits gingerly on the edge of the closest chair.

'You don't have much longer here."

"Yes. I would like more time to see the country and get to know the people. That means you most of all Margaret." He knows right away he shouldn't have spoken so openly. Her eyes grow big and her jaw drops slightly.

She stands up facing Henry and puts her arms above her head and then brings them over her chest, all the while staring angrily at him, as if to ward him off. He sees the silver ring slip noiselessly from her finger onto the rug. She makes a short excuse and hurries out the door. Before she closes the door, she turns and speaks quickly and formally. "I'll have the night girl leave a bundle of wood outside the door for your morning fire."

He stares absently at the ring on the rug.

Acch, I' din' another right mess. She'll not be bringin' me my grub for a few days. I be eating in the kitchen.' Na' so bad if I can see her.

He then bends and retrieves the ring from the floor. *I see it has no stone but a capital S and a W where the gem dinae be. Mighty fine silver this one. Mae fetch a few good pennies. I'll have to return it when a chance come to be seein' her again.* He places the ring in his trouser pocket. *Don't want me brother to be findin' it. Best keep it with me for now.*

Meanwhile, Arthur is cleaning up the last of the supper dishes. The area between the kitchen and the dining room is wide open. Against the wall of the dining room a warm crackling fire is burning. Mr. Holmes is sitting chatting to an older gentleman. They are sitting facing each other on either side of the fire. Arthur listens to the conversation.

"I say young fellow- Jack Holmes you said, I believe. You are from Scotland. What brings you to this wild country?"

Holmes hesitates, drawing on his pipe. He had recently taken up smoking a pipe. He coughs on the inhale, withdraws the pipe from his mouth and tries to think quickly. "Lovely country is it not,"

And then again, he says hurriedly "So what city in Nova Scotia did you say you were from?"

"We live on the outskirts of Halifax, between Halifax and Greenwich. Yes- my family has a country estate there. Orchard country. We grow apples and pears. Fine fruit growing country and we ship the fruit all over Canada and into the US."

"More cultivated. A better class of people I would think."

"Well, I wouldn't say exactly that."

" What is your name. sir?"

" Cameron, Alistair Cameron."

" Now you surely can't deny that's an aristocratic name."

" I am out west with my wife Lily to tend to business. I rather enjoy the colorful characters of this area. Never mind. We're not all alike and that's what makes life most interesting and rewarding."

Holmes, still trailing on about classes of people, gets up and faces the fire, supposedly to toss his pipe ashes in the fire. He makes a show of knocking the pipe against the side of the fireplace to loosen the ashes, then removes what appears to be several envelopes from his jacket pocket, looks around carefully, stoops towards to the fire and tosses them into the flames. Just then,

Arthur turns to wipe the kitchen counter. He sees Holmes throw what looks like three small brown envelopes into the fire.

When he returns to the back room, Henry notices something gnawing at Arthur.

Arthur twists his angular frame into the chair beside Henry.

"Wha's gettin' ta' ye?"

"It's Holmes. S-Startin' to s-see wha' you been s-sayin."

"Boasting at supper table again was he?"

"Y,' he always d-does that. I-I think he's tossed ta' let-t-ters in the f-fireplace."

"Wha'!- Yer spectacles are on sideways."

"Small brow-wn e-envelope like the one we put the let-t-ter to mum and father in. I w-was watching, He didn't see me t-there wi-i-pping the ta-b-bles. Three l-letters."

"Tis' our letter home and must be Stewy and Fred's letters too? What's this man up to? I thought he was a bit of a fool, nae he gittin' up to something no good. Din' he hopin' to cut our ties with our families back home?" He hesitates, furrows his brow and drums his knuckles on the hard wooden arm of the chair.

"Let's write an-nother letter home and mail it ours-selves," suggested Arthur.

"Good idea. What would we be sayin' exactly?"

***

Henry spends a restless night. He listens to the slow rhythmic drone of Arthur's snoring from the bed across the room. It soothes his tired brain.

Some things never change. But now what do we do? Go home as fast as possible before Holmes trips us up again? Say nothing to Stewy and Fred for now. They are only letters, they can be replaced, as Arthur said. The other touchy part is that Holmes has our money and our passports. I haf' ta' figure what I canna do to be fixin' that. He's out ta' jigger us up.

Henry sleeps fitfully for the rest of the night and finds himself awake early and staring out the window at the sun rising over the hills. The hush of the dawn's grey vapour slowly vanishes, and a soft blue sky appears above the meandering hills.

The mornin' is welcoming me. To wha' the blazes, I be knowin' soon. I see there a wee bit a' wind today. I'll go and have it out with Holmes before Arthur gets up. Dinna' be knowin' wha' be takin' me to his cabin with only a pair of wooden sticks?"

He hears a what sounds like a horse whinnying outside. He opens the back door and sees the empty hay wagon is parked outside, but with only one of the work horses hitched to it.

"Wha' the devil!" he shouts for all to hear.

Arthur wakes and stumbles to the open back door, running his hands over his unruly red hair.

"Wha' ch' makin' a din s-so early?"

Before Arthur can say another word, Henry hoists himself in the wagon, dropping the crutches in the dirt and snapping the reins, steering the horse towards Holmes' cabin.

Arthur stares after Henry. He opens his mouth to call his brother back, but it's pointless, as all he can see in the distance is a giant tumbleweed rolling happily along behind Henry in the fast disappearing wagon. He picks up the crutches and props them against the wall of the building, He sits with his head in his hands, his pyjamas flapping in the breeze on the wooden steps.

Tha' brother a' mine, off to see Holmes. Aye, he can fix it.

***

Henry stops the wagon in front of Holmes cabin. No sign of life. No lamp flickers in the window. He pushes on the door. It opens slightly and Henry steps over the sill. Then he sees it. Nothing. The cabin is completely empty, except for a clean oil lamp on the table. Nothing remains. Not a crumb of food, or a bit of ash from Holmes' pipe, or even a bit of paper on the wooden floor. Henry steps out and looks around half expecting to see Holmes strolling back from a morning walk, goin' on about someone important he'd met, or yarlin' on about the hay crop gettin' in.

Henry takes a step, forgetting that he had left his crutches behind, and stumbles across the clearing and grabs onto the reins of the old horse, as he is about to fall. He is holding the reins, but he stares past the horse.

Holmes has done a runner. He's done a right -damn runner on us. With our passports and money an' all. Wha' the blazes he gone? Musta' been fishin' out the train schedule yesterday when Still-Water dropped him off at the station. I feel a chillin' in my heart an' foot aches. I think this is what loneliness feels like. I wish to God I'd never left Scotland. Father was right in a way. Dangerous. Holmes is dangerous, not the damn Indians. Wha's he up to? I'll have to talk to Still-Water. Jack as Holmes pointed out to me yesterday. Jack it is.

Henry shakes his head and lets out a slow groan. The mare snorts and then sneezes, spraying Henry liberally. He steps back." Whoa, ye gettin' my attention. You know Hattie, old girl. Somethin' nae right here. Ha' ta' fix it somehow. Ye lost yer brother. You' be missing that old Billy- Boy beside you. " He puts his mouth up to her ear and talks softly. She in turn nuzzles his ear. "Best be off to the Inn."

***

Back in his small room, Henry shouts at Arthur who stands, uncomprehending.

"Will ya quit cleanin' for the love of God. Sit yerself and listen." Arthur puts down his dust rag and stares at Henry. "He's off, off I tell you. Acch- yer not hearin' me' man. Got to tell Still-Water."

Margaret who is listening at the door, steps inside the room.

"What -Who did what?"

"Holmes' off and taken Billy-Boy."

Henry relates the rest of what he has seen.

As Henry tells Margaret what's happened, she is jolted in to action. She quickly instructs Arthur to find her father and tell him what's happened.

Arthur finds himself in an adjourning field. They check out Holmes' cabin for themselves and find it deserted as Henry has said. They stand outside the cabin in the warm September sun. Arthur runs his fingers through his thick red hair. He shuffles his feet across the thin sandy soil. Jack is wearing a straight-cut suit with a waistcoat and a large cowboy hat.

"I'm part businessman and part, plain country farmer as you know." He takes his hat from his head and fans himself with it. "This is bound to set me back." Jack runs his hand across his sweating brow. He clears his throat and loosens his tie, then looks up at the tall young man.

"I'm with you boys. You'll all have to get the hay in, regardless, but I won't leave you stranded."

"Yes sir. We be gettin' the h-hay in. H-Holmes has gone off with yer horse. Wha' ye go-goin' do Mr. S-Still-Water?"

"I think Billy-Boy will find his way home," he says with a rueful smile starting at the corner of his mouth. "Horses don't ride trains as far as I know and as I am sure Holmes took the early morning train out of Ashcroft and is God knows where by now, Billy Boy likely was left hitched up at the station. I'll send a rider for him."

"J-Jack, we be in a mess. Shouldn't' a' come h-here with H-Holmes. We thinkin' he be good for wha' he says bein' ta' schoolmaster an' all. Taught us g-grammar and maths good as any master."

"We'll talk it out round the table later. Holmes is taking advantage of young men who naturally go looking for adventure. It seems likely he was in some kind of financial or personal trouble. His backer, who was essentially me as owner of this ranch, has paid his and your way to Canada. This it seems is what he was after. Good country to get lost in as it's such an undiscovered and undeveloped land. It's not your fault or Henry's, but like you say- a right damn mess."

Meanwhile back at the Inn, Margaret and Henry are having a quiet talk in Henry's room.

"I apologize f' speakin' out of turn t' other night.. As for bein' a farmhand, father is a Church of Scotland minister. We bein' well respected as a family."

"I apologize as well." Margaret blushed. "You took me by surprise. Let's stay friends then. That's best under these circumstances."

"Aye, yes.. Best under tae circumstances." He feels a gnawing in his gut. Henry mumbles. "Yes ye right." He suddenly remembers the ring he had hastily placed in the cupboard the other night. *I must return it to her today.* He cannot look at Margaret, so he stares blankly at his feet. Then he adds. "Do ye' think yer father be thinkin' of takin' me on fer the winter? We'll do up the hay right proper no matter. I be willin' to do chores- til the Spring and then move on. Maybe go on back home." He let a longing gaze flicker in her direction. It slips past the grip he is trying to keep on his emotions. Margaret averts her eyes to the space above Henry's head. Margaret is trying to focus their talk on what needs to be done.

"You'll need to ask him. He wants us in the house at 3pm. for a meeting."

"Odd- I feel glum- right glum- a wee bit hopeful at the same time."

She smiles briefly, inclines her ear towards the door, then gets up.

" I think I hear Billy- Boy out back."

They step outside.

Jack is stroking Billy Boy's mane. "They likely let him loose at the station figuring he'd find his way back to us. The farm boy must have opened the gate for him."

Billy Boy stamps his feet and whinnies impatiently.

"Yes, you clever fellow, we are so glad your home safe." Jack looks fondly at Billy and pats his flank. "You are a damn good working horse. Glad you found your way home to us."

"Wha'd' Arthur get off to?" Henry ventures.

"In the kitchen helping with dinner preparation. Good fellow, Arthur. Knows his way around a kitchen. He'll be cooking for us soon. You never know. The kitchen girl is teaching him to roll out pastry I believe."

"He be knowin' how to put up a pie crust, Sir. Used to help me mum out. Father be callin' him daft and chasing him out of kitchen but he always found his way back." He smiles at the memory of Arthur dodging their father to be spending time making pies and scrubbing the dishes. Jack, in spite of the day's setbacks, finds himself smiling widely at Henry's recollections of life in Selkirk with his family.

Jack checks his pocket watch inside his waistcoat.

"Yes, yes, charming story indeed, we need to get on here, Henry. I see you've let go your crutches. Still off balance a little. Healing well no doubt?" Without waiting for an answer, he asks, "Can you take Billy to the barn, brush him and see he has water and a few oats?" He looked at Henry directly, as if sizing him up for the first time. "Then come along to the house and we'll see what we can all work out."

"Yes sir. I'll be checkin' the other horses too."

"Thank you."

Maybe boss is thinking of askin' me to stay on and this is his way of findin' out if I know my way with horses, Henry thinks, *as he gently brushes Billy Boy's coat, waters and feeds him. Smart man that Jack. Time fer a proper letter home once we sort our business. I be makin' damn sure it's posted by m' own hand..*

Henry tends to the other horses looking at their feet. *Hafta remember to tell the boss to call in the ferrier to be checking out which ones need new shoes.*

Then he sits on the barn stool. He chews idly on a piece of straw and picks up a discarded newspaper thrown in the corner in order to wipe the soles of his boots before leaving the barn. Then he sees it. A short article at the bottom of the first page.

The headline reads. "Have You Seen This Man?" Holmes face mocks him from the crumpled page.

"Former Scottish schoolmaster Jack or John Rupert Holmes is wanted in the British Isles for fraud and possible embezzlement. He is not considered dangerous and not believed to be carrying a firearm. It is believed he has fled the British Isles. He may be traveling by train or horseback to the Canadian BC interior, accompanied by several young men. If anyone has information regarding his whereabouts or activities, please contact the local RCMP detachment in Kamloops."

Henry notices the paper was dated August 20th, 1908.

A day or two before we set 'erselves in BC. the law was trackin' im. I think we all been horn-swaggled. Mighty good word Margaret taught me. I' be showin' this to folks inside.

Henry grabs the newspaper and limps along to the house for the meeting. He washes his hands and face at the outside pump and then knocks on the door.

The others including Stewy and Fred are seated around the table. The younger boys are distraught and angry. Fred speaks "We got t' get home. You were right about Holmes, Henry. Right from the start, you were callin' him out."

"Please not now." Jack cautions Fred.

"Join us Henry."

Henry sits in the closest chair. Margaret is sitting next to him. He tries not to think about that. He hands the newspaper to Jack, who reads the article and puts the paper on the table.

"Damn bastard has the same first name as me." Everyone laughs.

" I'll be visiting the RCMP office in Kamloops in the morning and I'll be letting them know he was staying here at the Inn. I'll give them all the particulars they need. Stewy and Fred you're coming to town with me and we'll see about ordering new passports at the Federal Building. Dress smart and be at the front of the Inn by 7am. Once you have your passports, I'll get you both on the train and then the boat overseas and then home to Selkirk.

"May take several weeks to get you on the train from Kamloops, so you'll work off your passage in the meantime. You be sure to visit Henry and Arthur's parents once you're home and kindly let them know what has happened. I'll hold you to that, as I'll be getting their address and writing to them very soon. Sit down tonight each of you and write letters home. I want to see the letters first thing in the morning so don't seal them. We'll post them tomorrow if they're done right. If not, you'll do it again until they're done right. You tell your parents everything. Understand boys?"

"Yes Sir," they respond in unison. A titter of laughter fluttered round the table.

"I blame myself for what happened. I hired the

man without looking at his face. We were of course only able to correspond by letter. Never again will I hire anyone without the ability to look into their eyes. Because I consider it my responsibility I will try to rectify…"

Arthur interrupts. "W-Wha' all ha-appen, Jack?"

Arthur had asked the question everyone wanted to know the answer to.

"He left his cabin, took Billy-Boy, rode to Ashcroft proper and then caught the train from Ashcroft station sometime last night, taking with him all his possessions and the money he was holding onto for all you boys and all your passports. We have no idea where he is. It says in the paper he was fleeing crimes in Britain. You boys coming here to help with haying were just his excuse to get out of Britain."

"Henry been knowin' all along he was shifty bugger," Stewy began. "Y' shoulda' seen them spattin' in the Kamloops train Station."

"Never mind that now," Jack answers. He coughs and goes to speak again, but chokes on his words. He begins again. "This is hard on all of us. Now you two get off to the kitchen. The girl will have your evening meals wrapped up for you to eat in your bunkhouse and then get yourselves a good night's rest. See you bright and early. Off with you now."

The younger boys nod in ascent and leave

quickly.

Jack breaths a sigh of relief, then turns his attention to Henry and Arthur.

Margaret looks at her father with concern.

"Henry, you're a hard worker and seem to know what your doing in the barn and hay- field. You'll be in charge til' it's stoked and the rest stacked in the barn. About another week's work, I should think. The younger boys will miss tomorrow in the field but be back with you the next day on cutting.

"Thank goodness I hadn't given Holmes any of your pay packets yet for putting up the hay, so the young boys will be getting their money before I send them back off overseas. Do either of you have an idea of what you would like to do? I am not going to give either of you passage home as you both can work for it, that is if you'd like to stay on at the ranch, at least for the fall and winter season."

Arthur shuffles nervously and then speaks up.

"I mi-might get off to N-Nova S-Scotia, Jack. Means New S-Scotland. I dinae know. Alistair Cameron- he been askin' me 'bout workin' fer h-him. I be talkin' to him in the k-kitchen. He be thinkin' I don't need no b- boss or gaffer l-lookin' out after me. He smiles at Henry. You been a g-good boss in the hay-yin' but I don't need no g-gaffer in the k-kitchen. You g-gonna' be on at me Henry?"

"You havin' a laugh? Goin' across Canada. What about goin' home as we planned to mum and father?"

"D-Don't know yet, H-Henry. L-lots we d-don't know yet."

"Arthur," Jack coughs behind his hand to intercede. "We still have to decide. I'll have a chat with Alistair later to check out his intentions."

Jack turns his gaze to Henry. Margaret listens intently.

"Would you stay on for the winter and help with chores, whatever needs a hand? In the Spring you can sort yourself again. You should have enough for a passage home by then if that is what you wish. You're your own man now. You too Arthur. Time to see to life on your own terms. To cook your own goose and eat your own dinner, as it were."

"I'll stay on." He wants to look over at Margaret and has to grip the side of the chair to stop himself. He keeps his eyes on Jack.

"I must say, I am damn pleased Henry." He smiles and reaches over and shakes his hand vigorously. "We're done here today. Got a few things settled at least. He smiles again then sighs, bangs his fist on the table and then stands up and straightens his waistcoat. He glances down at his watch and heads towards the outside door off the kitchen. "Must be off." Before he goes out the door, he turns to face Margaret and the boys. "I must say, damn that Holmes, but maybe it'll all be for some good in the long run."

The next day Henry and Arthur take on the haying with gusto. With the help of a couple of boys from a neighboring ranch they manage a full day's work.

When the work was finished for the day, Henry and Arthur chat against the fence.

"You talk yet with Mr. Cameron?"

"No-N-not yet."

"Yer goin' so far away."

"Like J- Jack says we got ta' c-cook our own g-goose now."

Henry snickers and then laughs. A loud hearty laugh that rings across the field.

"Wha"s so funny?"

"I think the goose hae already been cooked... stranded in BC. with no passports and no passage home. Ha. Nae dinna mind'. Goose got up an' flew far away I say."

"You m-mean H-Holmes is the goose!"

Henry pokes at his chest.

"Watch it, yer makin' me-- l-laugh." Arthur laughs so hard he begins choking, he catches his breath, then begins again.

They both fall to the ground, doubling over. In the grips of crazy laughter, they begin chucking hay at one another. When they look up the boss is standing over them with a wry grin on his face. Henry stands up.

"Sorry sir. It's just that Holmes is the goose that got away." They tried to regain their dignity but laughter keeps sneaking up on them. Henry looks at Arthur who has a long piece of hay sticking sideways from his ear. "Yer lookin' like a daft scarecrow, brother." Henry reaches up and gently pulls the stalk from Arthur's ear. They brush the hay bits from their clothes.

"So this is how you boys relax after a day's work. I must say, fine job with the haying. Dam sight better than Holmes ever did. I must say, I'll suppose I'll be getting the joke about Holmes soon enough. I got the two boys sorted for now and got their letters posted to their parents. Their passports should be arriving soon and then they'll be off home. Arthur, come along with me then and we'll have that chat with Alistair. Damn fine man that Alistair. You won't be going wrong taking up with him. He has land and money but not given to holding it over anyone's head. Been damn fine having him as a guest. Come along then. Henry will finish up here."

After they leave Henry is overcome with sadness as he knows without a doubt, his brother will go with Alistair Cameron to work for him at his home near Halifax. *Such a long way across country. Ur lives ha' been changin' so quickly in a month a' being in Canada. Would they be seein' their wee mum, father or friends in Scotland again? I be savin' m' fare and be goin' home in Spring, if I be of a mind, as Jack said. I' be missin' me brother and me dear mum.*

Henry hitches up the horses to the hay wagon and slowly drives them back to the barn to settle them for the night.

One Month Later.

Henry waits on the train station platform with Arthur, Jack, Alistair Cameron and his wife Lily. They are all shivering in the chilly wind. Arthur is excitedly waving his ticket in the air.

"I'll be g-getting the next t-train wi' these fine folks. Sad to be leavin' y' b-brother. Y'll be g-ettin' on with Margaret, I ex-p-pect."

Henry shudders, but not from the cold wind. He shakes his head to indicate no, hoping no one will notice. Jack looks askance at Henry. He starts to speak, but Henry quickly interrupts.

"Don' be wavin' ticket around, brother. Wind el' catch and ye be staying the winter instead of Halifax like y' planning."

Lily and Henry trade knowing looks.

"Yes, yes, That would be a shame for all of us. Listen to your older brother." Lily smiles mockingly at Arthur. "We enjoyed your apple pie the other night. We're hoping you'll be making more of those for us in the coming months."

"Yes indeed. Jolly fine indeed." Alistair agreed.

Arthur stuffs his ticket in his coat pocket and beams at Lily. "I'll be makin' pies as long as yer gettin' them apples from orchard, Ma'am, I ahh-m- mean Mrs. C-Cameron. I c-cana live my life way I like. Nae f-father ch-chasin' me outa' the kitchen."

Everyone chuckles. Then the train hisses into the Ashcroft Station.

"We're all proud of you Arthur," added Jack. Even your brother here, likely wishing he didn't have to see you going so far away. You'd all best get on the train. You have several days travel ahead."

Henry steps up to hug his brother and whispers quickly in his ear.

"Dinna be speakin' out of turn."

Arthur looks puzzled, but doesn't answer. Then in a louder voice for all to hear, Henry continues, "Ye got your own smarts. Use em' and ye be makin' a good man in ye new life."

He steps back and grins playfully, then grabs him roughly in another hug before Arthur turns to leave.

"For n-now, my b-brother." These are the last words Henry hears Arthur speak facing him on the narrow steps to the passenger car, before he disappears inside. Henry sees Arthur flash a quick grin, then he is gone.

After all the goodbyes are said, the two men ride silently home to the ranch in Jack's model T. Eventually, Jack speaks from behind the wheel.

"What was the bit that Arthur mentioned at the station about you and Margaret getting on?"

"Aye, nothin.' Henry stares fixedly at his rough hands. "He bein' happy for me havin' company my age, and as Stewy and Fred left last week and with Arthur takin' his leave an' all. He's thinkin' kindly a' me is all."

"Of course, Yes, I see. I lost my wife several years ago to a sudden illness, so I understand you're feeling a little lost, but I must say, you'll find new friends and a good life here. My two older sons are returning from a trip abroad in a few days. You'll enjoy taking up with them." He pauses, then continues. "Another bit to think about, as I'm sure you already know, being only two months away from the old country. Our worth here does not come so much from our family name or our position in society. What there is here for a man to get ahead is his own guts, brains, skill and character. Who he is, is the making of him and if you plan to make a life here in BC, I must say, I can be a part of helping you get a lift up."

"Very grateful to you Sir."

" Ahh, forget sir and all that nonsense. Jack, Jack, if you please."

They ride in silence for a time. Henry looks out at the straight backed fir trees and the Ponderosa pines which draw nourishment from the sparse, dry, hillside beneath them. His thoughts drift back to lingering memories of summer hay-fields and foolish laughter with his brother. He looks up at the cold autumn sky.

Damn, dreamin' of Margaret, She dinae' seem to be far from me mind fer long. He sucks in his breath, so as not to speak his thoughts out loud. He glances over at Jack, feeling a sharp clutch of guilt in his chest.

Jack peers at the sky through the car's narrow windshield. "Starting to fog up. Looks like the snow's coming. I must say, she's hiding there inside those cold white clouds."

"Aye Jack. It surely be snowin' anytime and we need to be tendin' the horses before the snow be on em' tonight. Henry is quiet for a few minutes. Looking across at Jack he speaks again in a voice somewhere between asking and telling.

"I dinae' know Jack, but thinkin' I be keepin' a wee Aussie Shepard pup from the next litter. Be right good, come the Spring, to train im' up proper for herdin' new calves an' all."

Then he recalls the silver ring once again.

Still sittin' in the cupboard in me room. Margaret been askin' about if anybody's seen it. How I be explainin' this one? Another right mess be comin' my way.

Eileen lives in Kamloops, B.C., by the
North Thompson River where she enjoys
walking the dog. She has a messy garden
in the backyard in which she putters
about happily.

Contact Eileen through Celticfrog
Publishing at celticfrog@live.com

Other Published Works by Eileen Bell
Children's Books
Dog-Gone- 1992,1998

The Keeper of the Shell- 2019-Celtic Frog Publishing

Available on Amazon in hard copy or e-book

Soft cover available from Ingram Spark Publishing

Works in Anthology's
Short Stories- Polar Expressions Publishing- 2015-16

Poetry- Polar Expressions Publishing- 2013- 2016

Poetry Books
Eileen Bell and Friends- Overland Press-2017

River-land and other Poems- Celtic Frog Publishing-
2020

Available on Amazon

Eileen Bell is a regular contributor of stories and poems to the New Author's Journal- Mario Farina- Publisher-Quarterly Journal Available on Amazon in hard copy or e-book.

For other soon to be published works please refer to CelticFrogPublishing.com/Eileen-Bell.

www.ingramcontent.com/pod-product-compliance
Lightning Source LLC
Chambersburg PA
CBHW071351200726
48293CB00008B/2606